Who Will Believe
TiM KiTTEN?

by JAN WAHL
Illustrated by Cyndy Szekeres

PANTHEON BOOKS

To JENNIFER
and KIMBERLY

Text Copyright © 1978 by Jan Wahl
Illustrations Copyright © 1978 by Cyndy Szekeres Prozzo

Library of Congress Cataloging in Publication Data
Wahl, Jan. Who will believe Tim Kitten? SUMMARY: Tim Kitten has his great-grandmother's
talent for telling tales, but no one believes his stories. [1. Cats—Fiction] I. Szekeres, Cyndy.
II. Title. PZ7.W1266Wh [E] 77-12956 ISBN 0-394-83666-9 ISBN 0-394-93666-3 lib. bdg.
Manufactured in the United States of America. 0 9 8 7 6 5 4 3 2 1

CONTENTS

CHAPTER ONE
Little Fish Story

It was a mild, lazy, early spring Dawn. The sun gleamed like a bright apple hung by string. Hickory trees sprouted fresh, unfolding buds. Tim kitten padded with his father, Father Cat, down to the winding road.

The Iron Works, where Father Cat was head rat catcher, stood miles off. "Bye, Son," he called briskly, trudging to work.

Father Cat followed the groove of road over high bulging ground, until he was almost out of view.

Beside the road Tim found something oily and shiny. He wiped it on the grass, pushing it into his pocket. It was a secret.

"If I had an auto, I'd drive you," Tim yelled after his father.

"Well—think of that!" laughed Father, disappearing around a bend.

Slowly Tim shuffled back to the tiny

house which sat under an old boxcar, left forever in the weeds. Once the boxcar had belonged to a real freight train, traveling far, chugging and roaring down now-rusty tracks.

Tim flicked his tail with boredom. His sisters Hepzibah and Jessica were enjoying a mud fight. He wanted to do something too.

"If I had an auto, I'd whisk you to the seashore," he said.

"POOH!" cried both sisters. *Zap!* Tim ducked a mud ball.

He didn't feel like getting his clean fur dirty so he slipped inside, where his mother, Mother Cat, was washing breakfast dishes.

"If I had an auto, I'd take you out for a spin," announced her son.

"That's nice, Timothy," Mother sighed.

"Such a *sissy* name. Call me Tim," he grumbled.

"No, it's a marvelous name," smiled his mother, giving him a towel to dry with.

"You were named for Great-Grandmother Cat's brother. He was watchcat in a bookshop. He was a READER! He could recite *any* poem asked for," she revealed. Her eyes glittered with pride.

Of course Tim kitten would never forget his famous great-grandmother who

had had terrific adventures and bragged about them.

Yet he never heard of her smart brother. "What happened to HIM?" asked Tim— drying the same plate over and over.

Mother Cat replied sadly, "He got caught by a dog who couldn't read."

"Oh. He wasn't so smart, after all!"

Suddenly Tim decided, "Mom, I'd like to go fishing."

His mother excused him. Grabbing pole and fishing tackle, off he trotted full of Spring hopes. His sisters, with mud to the tips of their long tails, rolled gleefully in oozy slime.

"Jump *in* with us!" Hepzibah invited. However Tim was thinking of catching a nice, tasty, wiggly, fat fish. His mother would fry it with butter and flour and onions. How *proud* Father would be!

"Scaredy cat!" said Jessica.

Nobody ever took him seriously. Nobody guessed he'd do anything IMPORTANT!

Pretty soon he came to the bank of the pond fed by the stream leading down to the river that probably flowed into the Sea itself.

So—it was possible to catch anything. A minnow. A pickerel. A swordfish! Who knows *what* hid under the bright pond's ripples?

Tim tossed his line, *plop,* into the water—and settled down on the moss bank to wait. Maybe he'd catch a nice juicy eel. He licked his chops. He waited and watched pink and purple crocuses peep out of new, growing grass and a wren family building a nest in the beech tree above his head.

Everyone had something to DO!

Father Cat had his job. Mother Cat had chores about the house. Jessica and Hepzibah loved wrestling.

> *What is it I wish?*
> *To catch a fish?*
> Tim wondered.

Lying on the soft bank, he blew on a dandelion stem. Not even a minnow nibbled. Hey! A tug on the line.

Plip—out it flew—water squooshing. Ugh, an old rubber boot! Back he hurled the line.

Harold sauntered by with a fishpole. "Are they biting?" he asked.

"No," said Tim. His whiskers tingled. Now he had an audience.

"Harold, did I ever tell you about that time I had an auto?" He was getting warmed up.

"Are you fibbing again?" said Harold. "I'll bust you in the geezer!"

Tim put his paw in his pocket, taking

out the shiny object he'd found at Dawn by the roadside. He boasted, "Here's its *spark* plug. In fact—it was a racer!"

Forgetting about fishing, Harold became interested. A bee buzzed.

Tim began . . . "It was the Desert Classic! I wore goggles and kid gloves and shot right past cactuses till I came to a huge Mirage."

"Mirage? What's THAT?" asked Harold.

"Something seeming *real,*" Tim explained, "but isn't there." The bee listened.

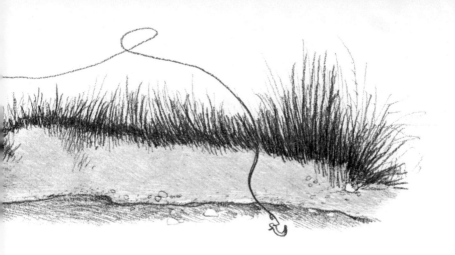

"Yeah! Like your stories," snorted Harold.

"I WON THE RACE!" insisted Tim.

"You couldn't win a race. You're just a big liar!" Harold replied, sticking his tongue out, picking up his gear in disgust, scurrying off, leaving Tim kitten sitting on the moss bank. The bee flew off.

The only thing Tim caught that day was the second boot, and he wore both of them home, *slish slosh,* so at least he didn't go home empty-pawed.

CHAPTER TWO
Santa's Trombones

Mother Cat was stitching curtains out of odd snippets of cloth she had, so no two curtains looked alike. Tim was helping—he was very handy with scissors. Hepzibah and Jessica, wearing baseball uniforms, guffawed and zipped out the door. Jessica wore a catcher's mask and Hepzibah carried the bat.

Today it was the girls' team, the Bloomers, against the boys', the Beezers. Tim just didn't enjoy games. Somebody won, somebody lost! Was that fun?

After his sisters left, Mother Cat took the pins out of her mouth, saying, "There's a thrill about winning, Timothy! When I was a kitten I won a roller-skate championship. See!"

And she showed him on a fine silver chain a pair of silver roller-skates so tiny they seemed a flashing mote in the air.

"All the rest of my life I guess I'll know the *thrill* of that moment!"

Tim snipped away with the scissors, grunting, "Can't roller-skate around here. There's no sidewalk!"

It was gooseberry tea time. The rusty tin kettle sang on the iron stove. The curtain-makers sat down, nibbling thistle cookies and drinking tea.

A knock at the door.

It was Louella Tabby, collecting used clothing for the Old Cats' County Home.

"Hello, Lou. I don't have clothing, but if I have any material from the curtains I'll

sew a fine housecoat," Mother promised.

And she did. Tim was the model. He was standing on a stool with the half-finished coat of patches when Father Cat entered in his handsome rat-catching outfit. He'd forgotten his rat bag.

"Who is THIS?" he queried.

"I was helping MOM," grumbled Tim. He snatched off the housecoat, and with flying fur, dashed away. Everybody believed he was nothing!

In a daze Tim ran till he was at the baseball lot behind Muller's abandoned Stone Quarry.

Very carefully cat fathers had smoothed the surface, covering it with sand.

"Which side will you join?" jeered Harold, the pitcher. *"Bloomers* or *Beezers?"*

"We don't want him!" chorused the Angora twins, Agnes and Florence, sneering.

Jessica and Hepzibah might poke fun at their brother yet they'd fight for his honor! Hepzibah picked up her long

bat—marching straight to Harold's nose.

"Can't you take a j-joke?" stammered Harold lamely. The Angora twins were silent.

Tim stopped at the border of the baseball field, saying to the bleachers, "I am remembering SOMETHING."

What? When Tim remembered, kittens came to listen, just as he did when Great-Grandmother told her stories.

Baseball players and those in the bleachers gathered, one by one.

Is it getting a crowd
That will make me proud?
wondered Tim.

He rubbed paws, beginning.

"It was The Great North Pole Race!

"For weeks I'd journeyed till I reached the highest point on the Globe. Santa Claus was there in his red suit. So was Mrs. Claus.

"A beautiful ice stand got built. And that's where the Clauses watched from. Hot dogs, popcorn, photos of many contestants were sold. Penguins paddled forth for a closer look."

One of the Bloomers, Lizzie, hooted, "Penguins don't live at the North Pole!"

A Beezer, Corky, broke in, "Tim, stick to what happened."

The tale-teller, Tim, shifted from one leg to the other, scratching his head.

"They were penguins," he explained. "On a holiday from the South Pole. Who's telling it—me or you?"

"Everybody *quiet!*"

"Get going!" came shouts. Even the Angoras and Harold were eager.

"The ice was thick and smooth," described Tim. "Like a frosty crystal mirror. You could see everything reflected, clear. So slippery! Fortunately I had snow tires with chains."

The crowd could feel the cold.

"My motor froze. A fire was lit to thaw it.

"Santa raised a popgun. You had to circle *around* the North Pole. It was striped like a candy cane. Mrs. Claus brought me a wool muffler she'd knitted herself. She screeched into my ear through howling wind, 'MERRY CHRISTMAS!'

"The popgun popped—the Race started!

"My car shot forward on a smooth stretch of ice. Whiskery walruses and seals clapped with flippers. I turned at a difficult curve—I spun!"

Tim's crowd gasped.

"Twirling like a polished top! So did the

other racers! We were all spinning, ice was flying, but I kept my eye on the Pole.

"I straightened my wheels, whizzing to the end of the course. I won the race!"

In triumph, Tim showed them—"*Here* is that medal!"

"Only a dumb *tin can lid,*" hooted Wilbur, a Beezer.

"He couldn't win a snail's race," shrieked Polly, a Bloomer. Harold the pitcher was laughing so hard he rolled on the ground over and over.

Sadly, Tim muttered, "NOBODY believes
me." He passed his sisters who were whis-
tling nervously and studying their toes to
keep from joining the merriment.

"You should have heard Santa's Trom-
bone Band playing when it was over,"
finished Tim.

"He's lying. As ever," added Hepzibah,
but under her breath.

"You bet. Shush!" said Jessica.

Their downhearted brother drifted home, hanging his head, scuffing the dirt beneath his feet.

He discovered Mother Cat up in a plum tree picking plums, piling them in her calico apron. Tim climbed the ladder and sidled over beside her on the heavy limb.

"Hold me close, Mom!" he whimpered. She stroked his fur.

CHAPTER THREE
Fight on Kite Hill

Mother Cat stirred a lot of sugar with water, vinegar, and butter, boiling it in a huge blue pan. When it thickened, it was taffy.

The Taffy Pull began.

Hepzibah, Jessica, and Tim smeared oil and butter over their paws. Father Cat smoked a cork pipe, reading *Rat-Catcher's Weekly,* from time to time glancing at the pullers, chuckling in amazement.

Taffy was stretched. Patted. Twisted. Folded, dribbled, smeared. How it glistened! Joyful kittens whooped, "Whee!"

The Hobbses (the gypsy family who lived in the boxcar above the Cats) were out gypsying.

Tim kitten envied THEM.

Surely he was meant for something more exciting than playing with taffy!

"TIM-OTHY!" Mother warned.

"Wasn't WATCHing," he meowed.

A great bulging taffy loop entwined Tim, sticking to fur. The more he tried loosening it, the more it stuck!

His sisters toppled. Taffy stuck on their fur too. Father Cat jumped, spreading newspaper on the floor.

He squeaked, "Leap on this!" But when they did, paper stuck to taffy and fur. You could not tell which kitten was which. Mother Cat leaned on the cupboard, weak with laughter.

The three kittens were dipped in a tub of water and thoroughly scrubbed. They hated water.

In an hour they were clean once more. Father Cat lit a fire. Soon they were dry.

Jessica hopped around singing "Happy Days Are Here Again." Hepzibah sang, louder, "Pop Goes the Weasel."

"Where is your brother?" asked Mother Cat, still cleaning up the mess.

They hunted and searched. He hadn't left the room! At last he was located—hiding in a cardboard box, paws over ears.

"I can't *think* with all this racket!" scolded Tim.

Hepzibah trotted over. She bent down, thinking herself. "What would you like to do? Play blindcat's bluff? Or touch football? Marbles?" Tim waggled *No.*

NOTHING sounded appealing.

"Well, I am going to visit Aunt Gertie," decided Mother Cat. "It's been enough hubbub for me—also!"

And she put on her cheesecloth cape
tied with a mouse tail. She winked. Now
it was Father's turn to entertain the kittens.

A nice brisk wind rattled the door as she
went out and blew her across the neigh-
borhood.

"What about making a kite?" drawled
Father.

"KITE, yippee!" squealed the girls.

Tim crawled out from the box. It didn't
sound horrible.

So the four set to work building the frame from light sticks. The girls were excellent whittlers. Father Cat balanced the tied sticks on his penknife.

It was perfect. "Who *tied* the sticks?" whistled Father in awe.

"Tim," somebody offered.

"Tim has a super sense of BALANCE," praised Father. "He must get it from Mother—because of her roller-skating." Tim blushed.

Now what to cover the kite-frame itself with? Father Cat pulled at his tufted ears. Sacrificing, he donated his collection of *Rat-Catcher's Weekly.*

Now what to fashion the tail from? There were scraps of cloth from the curtains and housecoat. Too late, they realized the *Rat-Catcher's Weekly* issue featuring a big picture of Father was glued right on the front of the kite. It was the time he was Champion Rat Catcher.

"Sorry," mewled Jessica. And "Me too!" sobbed Hepzibah.

Tim didn't speak. He slithered, ready to vanish into the cardboard box.

He was the guilty one.

"Why, I'm flattered to appear on it!" said Father. "Let's get *flying!*"

Fortunately, Mother Cat saved string. The girls hoped to knot the longest towline.

Above Cherry Hill, the highest hill, queer white gulls and black crows soared in the sharp gray breeze.

The "birds" whipped back and forth—kites!

Carefully the Champion Rat Catching Kite was carried tilted so it didn't rip in strong wind.

"Keep up your end!" shouted Hepzibah, afraid Tim might stumble.

Both girls held the towline, together. They were quick sprinters. Father Cat took the bottom of the kite—to toss it when the wind changed.

Harold, with Corky, running a box-kite, jeered at Tim, a lone, small figure with paws in pockets.

He bawled, "What if your dumb kite falls? How will *you* catch it?"

Immediately Tim replied, "You never heard of my Giant Tornado Kite that propelled my car to first prize at The Kansas/Wizard-of-Oz-Race? Hey, I KNOW ALL ABOUT KITES!"

"Hoo, I'll bet!" guffawed Harold, failing to see his low box-kite bump on the ground.

At that instant Father Cat and the girls got their kite aloft. The line unreeled. Their kite became a wee, darting speck, the highest in the sky.

"Not fair. You *fibbed!*" wailed Harold, looking at his smashed wreck. "You made me forget!"

Tim almost began to apologize—but guessed Harold might bust him in the geezer. So he put on a fierce, scary, tough face—showing his teeth. It only caused kittens, clustered around, to giggle. For a second he was pleased.

> *Is it a bit of laughter*
> *That I'm after?*
> wondered Tim.

Harold sprang at Tim, though Corky tiptoed away. Tim and Harold tussled and rolled atop Cherry Hill—noisily.

A lot of kittens felt Harold was a bully, so some rooted for Tim.

However, in the middle of the fight, Father Cat reached down, picking up Tim and Harold each by the scruff of the neck. They kicked while he carried them off.

"Maybe I was *winning*," yowled Tim.

"*You* ain't a WINNER!" hooted Harold.

Tim's sisters reeled in their kite featuring the picture of the Rat Catching Champ. Hepzibah blurted, "Tim's telling fibs again!"

"Yep," sighed Jessica, asking, "What can we do about it?"

"Make it *come true,*" said Hepzibah.

She yelled in a strong, loud voice, "Noodle-heads! Tim's building a new NEW Zero Eight Racer right now!"

Kittens gulped.

"We double dare you," added Jessica, "to race him next Saturday."

Harold stood there, fidgeting. It was a challenge. "Okay, I'll have *my* racer finished by then!"

This was too much for the Angora twins. Holding paws, they scurried home, quick as wind, to start on their machine.

CHAPTER FOUR
Gumdrop and Balloons

Tim kitten sat indoors with a jigsaw puzzle while behind black hawthorn bushes his sisters hammered, punched, clanked, buzzed, and banged on Zero Eight.

Hepzibah and Jessica asked Tim to stay out of sight. Tim's mother sneaked them sardine cake and a thermos of mouse juice.

"Won't, won't, WILL NOT drive it!" he muttered.

At a furious rate kittens crossed the grass with wheels and bolts and nails— assembling race cars from scraps.

The Angora twins, Agnes and Florence, constructed, from a page torn from a book, a Catnip Double Seater. They fixed it night and day. Only forty hours till Saturday!

Mother Cat shook her head at her son. "You'll disappoint the girls," she pleaded.

"Humpf!" was Tim's answer, wishing

he could wiggle out of it. Oh, to skedaddle *beyond* the Iron Works—to see the World! How he envied starlings who flew hundreds of miles! Or eels . . . journeying from pond to stream to inlet to river to marsh to bay to endless Sea!

Rolling down a steep hill in a silly homemade jalopy was hardly the same.

But on Friday afternoon Tim grew curious and slipped off to the secret spot in the bushes where his sisters tinkered.

Hepzibah tightened a bolt with a monkey wrench. Jessica painted a bursting sun face and the numbers 0 and 8 on the side of Zero Eight.

Very impressive!

Having glimpsed it, Tim felt much worse. He just made up stories. Truly, that's all he could do!

The girls were tired. "Ask Mom to sew up a crash helmet," urged Hepzibah.

Jessica's tongue hung out of her mouth

as she concentrated on painting. She was
inspired.

"You're doing a swell job," said Tim.
"This is a Zero Eight, huh?" He touched
the fender. It was sticky.

"Won't be dry enough by tomorrow, I
suppose. Too bad!" he tittered.

That was too much for little Jessica.
With the tip of her brush she dabbed a
dot on his nose. "Okay Tim, *be* a clown."

That night Tim lay in bed positive he wouldn't sleep. His sisters snored away. Yet, before he knew it . . .

Coast to coast he was racing in a pure gold ZERO NINE *fast as lightning, silent as an eagle feather! Crowds thronged along the road—even on mountaintops and inside long tunnels.*

In the dark, people held candles. At the Finish—of course Tim was first—flags blazed his name. Wearing a white suit, the President himself bestowed the medal—a gumdrop with a diamond.

Mother Cat was shaking Tim.

It was only a dream. Miserable, he huddled under the blanket.

"Wake up, it's RACE day!" she purred. She brought a cup of hot chocolate.

Outside, sunrise was breaking, pink and orange. Mist hung over wet cold turf. Jessica and Hepzibah wore green coveralls.

"*Hurry!* The others are lining up!"

They pulled Tim outside. In front, by
the gate, sparkled a gorgeous Zero Eight.
The paint *had* dried. He rubbed both eyes.
"Hop *in!*" his sisters urged.

With a twinkle, Father Cat wished,
"Best of luck today, Son!" Mother Cat
gave him a shiny penny. His parents and
sisters pushed him up Cherry Hill.

There, vendors sold brilliant balloons. Kittens sat in cars and many cats watched.

Harold's nifty car was Tiger 1, assembled from an orange crate. His mechanic, Corky, gave him a pep talk. Stubby Whiskers was flag man.

Halfway down the hill, Mother and Father Cat mingled in the crowd with banners.

"Whoever rolls the farthest wins. Now GO!" signaled Stubby.

Jessica gave the auto a hard shove.

Down. Down it rattled, whirring. All at once Tim loved the racing sensation and he steered, zooming past the pit stop where Hepzibah waved encouragement.

"Go, Tim. Go!"

On rolled 08 as if by magic.

Agnes and Florence, the Angora twins, hit a rock and their Catnip Double Seater

lost an axle. Tiger 1 took Harold neck-and-neck alongside Tim. His sisters made his dream come true!

Harold seemed surprised to see Tim doing well. Among sycamore, beech, dogwood, maple trees the racers dodged.

Right across a wild field of mustard plants and a flock of butterflies.

Straight over rusty train tracks! Happily no train roared anymore but o8 and Tiger 1 just missed a handcar.

Is it worth being a winner
And losing your dinner?
Tim wondered.

On and on Harold's and Tim's cars
sped—the only two left—rattling—rolling—slower and slower.

Skillfully, Tim steered his machine over
dandelions, daisies, buttercups. The pant-
ing crowd followed, cheering.

"I don't have brakes!" Tim shouted. "I
don't either!" yelled Harold—and into a
tall yellow haystack both Tiger 1 and 08
plowed. Farmer Pangle came rushing up
with a pitchfork. When the two finally lay
uncovered it was Tim by an inch.

Sobbing, Harold kicked his auto.

Farmer Pangle's Jersey cow Myrtle
towed the winner home.

There was wild wild celebrating and
Mother and Father Cat wept with pride.
Stubby Whiskers polished the victor's cup
with a checkered hanky.

Tim pushed it away, crying, "I can't accept this. I know how it feels to win. But the truth must be told. I OWE EVERYTHING TO MY SISTERS!"

Balloons drifted skyward in surprise. Tim meowed softly, "Give it to Harold."

Weary but relieved, he sank down on pigweed.

Mother Cat squeezed Tim's paw, bragging, "Tim, you are a real winner. Telling the truth!"

And Father Cat quietly shook Tim's other paw.

Jessica and Hepzibah gave their brother a smooch. A figure lingered by the gate. Farmer Pangle.

The old fellow chuckled, "Turnips 'n' tarnation! That's *somethin'!*" He whispered to Mother and Father who fetched a pail and stool while Myrtle stood mooing.

As a gift, Pangle milked his cow. Soon the pail slopped with rich, tasty milk. The cream was scooped off for Tim, who waved it away.

He was busy lying on his back looking at a cigar-shaped cloud above.

Dreamily he asked, "Did I ever tell you about my *airship?* The Ace Platinum Golly-Wox Around the World Dirigible?"

His sisters, who were busy lapping up wonderful cream, stopped. The grownups stopped. Kittens gathered to listen.

"This story is true."

Nobody doubted him.

JAN WAHL studied folk literature and film at the University of Copenhagen, where he also worked with Isak Dinesen and film director Carl Dreyer. Since 1962 he has been writing exclusively for children and has over forty books to his credit. Mr. Wahl travels widely and makes regular trips to Mexico from his home in Toledo, Ohio.

CYNDY SZEKERES is the well-known creator of a host of captivating animal characters which have appeared in her numerous picture books including *Pippa Mouse, Maybe, a Mole,* and Jan Wahl's *Dr. Rabbit's Foundling.* She is also the creator of the popular Cyndy's Animal Calendar. A graduate of Pratt Institute, Cyndy lives with her family on a farm in Putney, Vermont.